Her Flash

Edited by Black Pear Press

With contributions by the entrants in the 2020
Worcestershire Literary Festival
Flash Fiction Competition

Thanks and acknowledgements to Judges:
Prof. Rod Griffiths
Dr. Tony Judge

This anthology is brought to you by
The Worcestershire Literary Festival
Flash Fiction Team www.worcslitfest.co.uk

Black Pear Press

Her Final Goodbye
Flashes from LitFest
Worcestershire Literary Festival
Flash Fiction Competition Anthology 2020

First published in November 2020
by Black Pear Press
www.blackpear.net

Copyright © Contributors 2020

All rights reserved.

Compiled & edited by:
Black Pear Press

No part of this publication may be reproduced, copied, stored in a retrieval system, or transmitted in any form or by any means without prior permission in writing from the copyright holder. Nor may it be otherwise circulated in any form or binding or cover other than the one in which it is published and without conditions including this condition being imposed on subsequent purchasers.

All the characters in this publication, other than those clearly in the public domain, are fictitious and any resemblance to real persons, living or dead, is purely coincidental.

ISBN 978-1-913418-25-0

Cover Design by Black Pear Press

LitFest & Fringe Flash Fiction Competition 2017.
Paperback ISBN: 978-1-910322-53-6
eBook ISBN: 978-1-910322-54-3

A Cache of Flashes 2016
Winners and selected entries from the Worcestershire LitFest & Fringe Flash Fiction Competition 2016.
Paperback ISBN: 978-1-910322-39-0
eBook ISBN: 978-1-910322-40-6

A Stash of Flashes 2015
Winners and selected entries from the Worcestershire LitFest & Fringe Flash Fiction Competition 2015.
Paperback ISBN: 978-1-910322-20-8
eBook ISBN: 978-1-910322-21-5

Fifty Flashes of Fiction
Winners and selected entries from the Worcestershire LitFest & Fringe Flash Fiction Competition 2014.
Paperback ISBN: 978-1-910322-10-9
eBook ISBN: 978-1-910322-11-6

Flashes of Fiction 2013
Winners and selected entries from the Worcestershire LitFest & Fringe Flash Fiction Competition 2013.
Paperback ISBN: 978-0-9927755-1-3
eBook ISBN: 978-0-9927755-3-7

A Flash of Fiction 2012
Winners and selected entries from the Worcestershire LitFest & Fringe Flash Fiction Competition 2012.
Paperback ISBN: 978-1-2911065-6-5

eBook and paperback first published by Crown East Publishing 2012 now available via Black Pear Press

Anthologies from Black Pear Press
Short Stories:

On the Day of the Dead and Other Stories
A collection of stories is taken from selected entries to the second Black Pear Press Short Story Competition, which took place during 2016.
Paperback ISBN: 978-1-910322-41-3
eBook ISBN: 978-1-910322-42-0

Seaglass and Other Stories
A collection of short stories from various authors in the first Black Pear Press short story competition 2014.
Paperback ISBN: 978-1-910322-14-7
eBook ISBN: 978-1-910322-15-4

Short Stories from Black Pear—Volume 1
A collection of short stories from Worcestershire-base authors including humour, true life, science fiction, horro and some almost impossible to categorise.
Paperback ISBN: 978-0-9927755-0-6
eBook ISBN: 978-0-9927755-2-0

Flash Fiction:

The Jar Thief—Flashes from LitFest
Winners and selected entries from the Worcestersl LitFest & Fringe Flash Fiction Competition 2019.
Paperback ISBN: 978-1-910322-17-8

Sacrifice—Flashes from LitFest
Winners and selected entries from the Worcester LitFest & Fringe Flash Fiction Competition 2018.
Paperback ISBN: 978-1-910322-89-5

Wired—Flashes from LitFest
Winners and selected entries from the Worceste

Competition Winners

In previous years the winners have been announced at the June launch event of the annual Worcestershire Literary Festival. Coronavirus restrictions during 2020 prevented the festival from being held in the usual manner, so, this year, the Worcestershire Literary Festival Flash Fiction Competition 2020 and the Flash Fiction Team announced the winners at the launch of 2020's virtual Worcestershire LitFest on 13th September.

The top ten flashes (alphabetically by title) were:

A Diamond Moment—Jan Baynham
False Impressions—Yvonne Clarke
Her Final Goodbye—Georgina Bull
Hungarian Red— Fritz Cavelle
Into The Sea— Rebecca Klassen
Smoke Without Fire—Susan Howe
The Champion—Kathryn Barton
The shoplifter— Roz Levens
Watching— Holly Yuille
Wonderin' about Jack and Diane—Roz Levens

From these, Judges Rod and Tony awarded:

First prize to Georgie (Georgina) Bull—*Her Final Goodbye*
Second prize to Yvonne Clarke—*False Impressions*
Third prize to Susan Howe—*Smoke Without Fire*

These stories are the first that appear in this anthology followed by those that were selected by the BPP team.

Introduction

We celebrate the ninth year of the Worcestershire LitFest and Fringe flash fiction anthology. The competition, founded by Lindsay Stanberry-Flynn in 2011, continues to be a popular event in the annual flash fiction calendar.

The anthology contains selected flash fictions entered in the competition, and we at Black Pear Press feel privileged to be asked by LitFest to compile, edit and publish it.

Prof. Rod Griffiths and Dr. Tony Judge read all the anonymised entries and made the tough decision to select winners.

The judges look for well-written and entertaining stories. They always say 'flash fiction is a difficult craft to master' because writing a story with a beginning, middle and end, within 300 words, is quite a feat. For a flash to be satisfying, every word must count.

Our winners exceeded the judges' expectations, as you will see when you read their pieces in this anthology. Congratulations to Georgie (Georgina) Bull, who took first prize with 'Her Final Goodbye'. Yvonne Clarke gained second prize with 'False Impressions'. Susan Howe took third prize with 'Smoke Without Fire'.

Thank you to every entrant for sending your flashes in to this competition. We know that it takes courage to have your writing judged by others. A final thank you to all the LitFest flash fiction team for your sterling work behind the scenes and, in particular, for rising to the extra challenge of holding a competition during the 2020 coronavirus lockdown.

Black Pear Press Limited
www.blackpear.net

Contents

Anthologies from Black Pear Press	iii
Competition Winners	v
Introduction	vi
Contents	vii
Her Final Goodbye—Georgie (Georgina) Bull (first)	9
False Impressions—Yvonne Clarke (second)	10
Smoke Without Fire—Susan Howe (third)	11
A Diamond Moment—Jan Baynham	12
Hungarian Red—Fritz Cavelle	14
Into the Sea—Rebecca Klassen	15
The Champion—Kathryn Barton	16
The Shoplifter—Roz Levens	17
Watching—Holly Yuille	19
Wonderin' About Jack and Diane—Roz Levens	20
A Different Plane—Anne Cuthbert	21
A Fitting End—Helen Beckett	22
A Good Old Rodeo Never Hurt Anyone—Anne Howkins	23
Always the Princess Aurora—Safia Sawal	24
A Mind at Peace—Claudia Saalmueller	25
Birds of Poland—Jenny Woodhouse	26
Chewed-up Nails and Dandelion Clouds—Jamie D. Stacey	27
China White—Fritz Cavelle	28
Cold Fish—Anne Cuthbert	29
Fox—Sheila Blackburn	30
Freudian Slip—Helen Beckett	32
Good for What Ails You—Lynn Ramsson	33
Hey, Lady!—Anne Cuthbert	35
Hitching Down the M5—Bronwen Griffiths	36
Lilith and the Half-Cut Magician—Mark Kilburn	37
Maternal Instinct—Susan Howe	39
Moon Mamas of the Silk River Nostoi—Mark Kilburn	40
More Than the Words You Left Me—Jamie D. Stacey	42
Octopi—Catherine Cruse	43
Remember the Murdered Man—Safia Sawal	44
Repeat Patterns—Susan Howe	45
Singapore Green—Fritz Cavelle	46
…So,—Mark Rogers	47
So Long Solar—Simon Linter	49
The Heatwave of 1957—Safia Sawal	50
The Man I Love—John Holland	51

The Monument—Charlotte Pinkney	52
The Tale of Hickory Dickory—Polly Caley	53
The Voices Inside—Kevin Brooke	54
Thoughts of a Woman Scorned—Jan Baynham	56
Toast—Rebecca West	57
Tumbling Sailor—Roz Levens	58
Unravelling You—Georgie Bull	59
Unsleeping the Dead—Bronwen Griffiths	60
Via Dolorosa—Brian Comber	61
Virgin Territory—Helen Beckett	62
What is in Your Fridge?—Steve Clough	63
When Falling Over becomes Having a Fall—Brian Comber	64
Woman Driving, Man Sleeping—John Holland	66
Authors' Biographies	67

Her Final Goodbye—
Georgie (Georgina) Bull (first)

The rain lashed so heavily against the window that Florence was afraid it would break. She pulled her blanket up to her chest and huddled down.

The storms had come first, then the climate refugees as the little seaside towns were swept away.

Florence picked up the brochure on her coffee table. The photograph on the front was of her new home, if she chose to move. The apartment was one of a hundred gleaming white pods in a skyscraper that looked like a bunch of grapes and reached beyond the clouds.

The old lady slowly pulled herself to her feet and shuffled across the dusty, dirty floor in her slippers. Florence ran her gnarled old hands over the carved wooden mantelpiece; over the bookcase and the little coffee tables that Grandpa had built so long ago.

She recalled those long summer days in her youth, playing hide and seek with her sister; Mama pinning her hair at the vanity table; Daddy and Grandpa carving the intricate designs on the fireplace. This house felt like the last living link to her family; they lived in the wood, in the furniture and in the walls.

But it would all have to be left behind.

Florence stepped out into the garden. Freezing water came up to her ankles, but she plodded on. Years ago, she had carried a small wooden coffin down to the bottom and planted a little painted wooden cross, then stood in the rain for hours, too numb to feel the cold.

The cross had blown away, but Florence knew where her daughter rested. This exact spot haunted her dreams.

If she left this house, she might finally be free of Angel's ghost.

In a whisper lost to the wind, the old lady said her final goodbye.

False Impressions—Yvonne Clarke (second)

'Look away,' she said to her daughter, exuding thinly-veiled disgust. Pursing her painted lips in distaste, she pivoted her eight-year-old daughter so that her back was to the door, the king penguin protecting its chick.

The red and black graffiti on the door next to the bus stop was explicit and crudely drawn, nothing like a Banksy, which even she had to admit had some artistic merit. Graffiti has turned every building into a blank canvas of late, she huffed. This area in particular had become a breeding ground for vandals and hooligans. She couldn't bear to live in this den of iniquity any longer, she thought, rootling industriously in the subterranean depths of her handbag until she found her latest lottery ticket. '*You* are our passport to a better life,' she breathed reverentially, imbuing the numbers with a responsibility they were unlikely to be able to fulfil.

A nattily-dressed young man was ahead of them in the queue. He looked out of place. She subconsciously stood taller and sucked in her stomach. What was he doing here? Tall, good looking, smart. Clearly a 'Better Class of Person'. Clearly not from these parts.

The number three bus veered into the bus stop, heedless of the puddles which reared up in muddy waves and cascaded onto the kerb, spattering those in the queue. Everyone surged forward, a scrum of bodies, all sense of propriety abandoned. Not so the smart young man. Stepping back, he treated her to a broad, lopsided grin. Good teeth. Nice eyes.

'After you, madam.'

Gratified and not a little flattered, she and her daughter boarded the bus. *That's* more like it, she mused inwardly.

The young man followed them onto the bus, tucking two spray cans deeply into his cashmere coat pocket.

Smoke Without Fire—Susan Howe (third)

The smell of smoke roused her again. She listened to Ray's snores and the vibration of the city nine floors below. Had it been a dream? No, it was as real as on all the other nights. If anything, it was growing stronger.

She swung her legs out of bed and padded to the window. There was no sign of fire. Through the opening, a familiar blend of exhaust fumes and wet dust wafted in.

The kitchen, drabber than ever in the dull yellow glow filtering up from the streets, yielded no further clues. She'd switched everything off before bed as usual, not trusting Ray with the responsibility.

She turned the keys in the outer door and drew back the bolts that protected them from the gangs cruising the building at night. A solitary light bulb flickered in the passage but nothing worse than the combination of urine and disinfectant assailed her. Wrinkling her nose, she closed and locked the door.

Smoky vapours clung to her skin as she stumbled back to bed. Soon the mustard fog shrouding the horizon would cool to grey as dawn crept closer. Soon after that, the alarm would signal the beginning of another empty day, unfulfilled by a monotonous job and an indifferent spouse.

As she lay down for a final half hour of rest, the fumes settled around her again. And at last she understood; she was the source. Smouldering away to nothing. The charred husk of what she might have been. A low moan escaped her throat.

Ray grunted and half-opened one eye.

'What's up?' he muttered.

She waited. Within seconds his snores confirmed his lack of any real concern.

A sliver of daylight appeared between the curtains as she reached for the suitcase. Already the air smelled much fresher.

A Diamond Moment—Jan Baynham

Edith looked at the display of Diamond Wedding cards along the mantelpiece, a lump forming in her throat. Sixty years. It should be one of the happiest occasions in her life and they always said they'd throw a big party. A true romantic, Frank always remembered anniversaries, presenting her with flowers or chocolates or little presents. He chose appropriate gifts to match the 'big' anniversaries, too. Edith's hand strayed to touch one of the earrings he'd surprised her with five years before. Beautiful emerald earrings, the stones rare like the length of their marriage.

'To match your eyes, girl,' he'd said when she'd protested they were far too expensive. 'Nothing is too much for my Edie.'

He'd be so excited at sharing this milestone in their marriage, loving nothing more than a big family get-together. But there would be no diamonds for this anniversary. No party. Not even a card. Tears burned along her eyelids.

Edie took a deep breath before entering the communal sitting room. She walked over to where her husband sat, motionless, staring into space.

'Hello, love. Happy anniversary.'

As always, two empty lifeless pools stared back at her. She could have been anyone.

Edie handed Frank a photo of a young bride and a handsome young man in uniform.

'Do you know what day it is, Frank?'

Nothing. He stared at the photo, then handed it back. Edie left it for a while. She tried again, placing the photo back into his gnarled fingers.

'It's a very special day,' she said.

Frank studied the photo intently until the corners of his eyes crinkled as he smiled.

'That's my Edie!'

Tears streamed down Edie's cheeks. By taking Frank back sixty years, she'd got the best anniversary present of all.

Hungarian Red—Fritz Cavelle

Fate brought me here. Sat me at a table in the shadow of the Opera House with coffee, brandy and cigarettes.

Then you came: striding into the square, drawing the soft spring sunlight in your wake. The surroundings seemed to bow their Art Nouveau curves to the curl of your hennaed hair. The cotton white of your shift shifted through the shallows of your form. Your smile cut like a blade to my core. And when the ice blue of your eyes met the black in mine: we knew.

You laughed like a docker, swore like the Pope and flashed warning frowns whenever I sounded inane. You leant to the Left, though you came from the Right, and your English rose cheeks glowed like porcelain at wrongs gone unanswered. Your beauty crushed me.

And your genius taught me: wine, words and politics, as you swayed through Pest's alleyways revealing their architecture, and bullet holes.

You skinned a knee on Buda's hills, the blood speckled sharp and bright. You sang to a wizen gypsy on Elizabeth Bridge then bought her last rose. That day, when the thunderstorm drove us to drink. That night, when the Danube ran in a silver shoal. My lips to the nape of your neck. Champagne in your navel, strawberries between your toes. That Sunday morning smile.

Those summer months were the best of this life.

I loved you. I loved you. I am sorry I bit you. I am sorry you're dead. But to continue I needed your soul.

Now I am complete, I'll return to the soil and sink into the dark arms of my home. And I will dream of you and your light until your image fades. Then I shall rise again and trust that Fate has found another you.

Into the Sea—Rebecca Klassen

Ivy watched the sea under the pre-dawn sky. She'd promised herself years ago that she would be here; the day after her husband had closed his strikingly pale green eyes and was in the ground. She'd promised to come and take on the water.

Best do it quick before interruption. But her mind journeyed back to yesterday's funeral. Pews had heaved with shaking shoulders and whispered kind words. Ivy had thought only of the beach.

At the wake, Ivy had spotted Janet. The pair had never lived more than ten miles apart since they were children. Best of friends, they'd holidayed together every year with the husbands and Janet's son, Tom.

'What will you do, Ivy? Now he's gone?' Janet had wept. Ivy had thought of the waves, her forty-year marriage over.

Janet had held her breath before saying, 'I don't know what *I'll* do.'

Then Tom had appeared next to her. Now a young man, with strikingly pale green eyes.

The waves lapped closer as Ivy recalled the day it had become clear. When Tom, a baby in his highchair, had looked at her with his father's eyes. The previously unexplainable had then been explained. Unmade beds, extra teacups, her husband's peculiarly silky voice through the wall on the phone. Ivy had gone home, pounded her pillow and screeched her vow.

'When that devil is buried, I promise to dance naked for joy in the sea!'

Now wet sand was between her toes and her clothes thrown to the dunes. Fresh breezes in new places and her hands up to the gradually brightening sky. Her feet plunged into icy waves, kicking up twinkling droplets and arms composing an imaginary celebratory song.

She danced and made another promise. That this wouldn't be her last dance.

The Champion—Kathryn Barton

Her after-lunch nap over, it's time for a cup of tea. That dratted pen pusher should be here by now. Anthea knows she doesn't need help, but the family, despite her wardened flat and personal alarm system, insists on assessment. When the do-gooder turns up, she can put the kettle on.

The building's entry-phone buzzes, Anthea presses the door-opening thingy. You're supposed to check who's there, but no one speaks clearly nowadays so what's the point?

The door to the flat opens. A bulging jute bag enters, propelled by a woman with a face like a wet weekend. Anthea, adopting her confused-but-sweet old lady persona, points her in the direction of the tea bags. Tea making for the old is obviously not on the social-worker course. The visitor clatters and fidgets, spills water on the worktop and sugar on the tray.

Anthea returns from a bathroom visit to find the woman in front of her shelf of silver cups. 'Shouldn't you get your wretched forms out? Let's get this assessment over.'

'Shut up, you doddery old cow. You pension-fat oldies are all the same. Never check who's at the door, do you? Never think it might not be who you expect. Far too smug. Now, I'll just put these sparkly things in my bag while you get your money. And don't tell me you haven't got any squirrelled away.'

She reaches for a trophy. Anthea turns away. Another cup is taken. Anthea pivots, one straight leg scything through arthritic pain, one stiffened hand chopping.

The unconscious woman makes an untidy heap on the carpet. Anthea's body will protest the exertion later, but she feels remarkably good. If the thief had stopped to read the engraving on the cups, she might not have tangled with a retired National Police Martial Arts Champion.

The Shoplifter—Roz Levens

During lockdown, I'm trying to keep fit—improve my core stability, lower my blood pressure, increase my metabolic rate, that kind of thing. I started with walking the dog—in my allocated exercise hour, of course. I'm very responsible. Every day I get fractionally faster, pant a little less at the top of the hills; knock another few seconds off my time. I've started jogging on the spot in front of 'Flog It', running through the advert breaks, doing burpees during weather forecasts.

I find I can do household stuff more easily, too. I swung the sofa out of the way so I could vacuum under it. I moved the furniture around so that I could put my desk in front of the window.

I'm really pleased with how it's all going. I've not lost weight, really—maybe a pound or two—but I've toned up. My bingo wings have disappeared. My jeans are looser.

I just feel different.

The garden's looking nicer. I demolished the old shed, and dug the concrete base out. I've planted potatoes, carrots, parsnips and spinach.

My husband laughed, somewhat nervously, when I told him about the spinach.

'Look at you!' he said, his voice squeaking a little. 'You used to be Olive Oyl. Now you're turning into Popeye.'

'I yam what I yam', I said, grinning.

Today, during my regulation exercise, I found 50p in my pocket—one of those nice ones with Paddington Bear on it. Only I dropped it. It bounced across the street and slid under the crumbling wall of what used to be the bookshop on the corner of the High Street. So I thought, 'If I can just get a grip on this brick…'

Seems like I don't know my own strength. They're charging me with shoplifting.

Watching—Holly Yuille

Sometimes it's just the colour of the sky. You wake up and the sky looks wrong. That's when you realise something's happening. Not long after that they start up, like clockwork figures in a Swiss model village, only never quite the same each day. At first, I knew everything that would happen. Then bit by bit it unravelled.

How long has it been now? The morning comes and dread pulls me like a rope towards the window. I lean my forehead towards the glass, breathe clouds, close my eyes and hope that when I open them the pane will be completely white and I won't be able to see.

My first girlfriend hated ants. The very thought of them made her itch. But the worst possible thing was to stamp on them, to lay down white powder in the corners of the room. The only thing worse than an ant was a dead ant, a vengeful ant. In many ways I feel the same. I imagine running down there, into the middle of the square and screaming, batting them away with my arms, but the dread of one slowly making its way towards me, smiling, touching my shoulder, looking into my face, it makes me shudder.

At some point the colour of the sky changes again and I come away from the window, my eyes trailing till the last moment to make sure nothing has changed.

I hear a click and a call from downstairs. The one that lives here is back. She'll be carrying an armful of shopping bags. She'll be taking off her uniform and putting on her pyjamas. She'll want me to go downstairs and put food in my mouth, to talk, to sit with her and watch them all again through the flickering electrical window.

Wonderin' About Jack and Diane—
Roz Levens

It's restful, a kick wheel. It builds up the muscles in one leg, rather, so trousers never hang quite right, but the rhythm and whirr are hypnotic. Somehow the hands moulding the clay are disconnected from your body, from the kick and spin of the wheel. You kick in time to the music on the radio and let your mind run free, listening to the stories in the lyrics, drifting along imagining what 'Ruby-Ruby-Ruby-Ruby' looks like, whether Jack and Diane ever made it.

Anything rather than think of the bills, the rows, the lack of orders.

The phone rings, but you can't answer, can't disturb the stack of this pot—the best one, the biggest one you've ever managed. You kick, and hum, and watch your hands, watch the wonderful pot grow. This one, this time, will be perfect. It will be the one you make your name, your fortune, your future on. There's a crash on the door as the bailiffs announce themselves. Your concentration wavers, and the pot, like your hopes, collapses in front of your eyes.

A Different Plane—Anne Cuthbert

Aliens were trying to communicate with her through the slot where you shoved used paper towels. It made sense, didn't it, hearing extraterrestrials when you were above the earth? They'd be outside, maybe in small craft or clinging to the fuselage. Perhaps they had suction pads—maybe their limbs *were* suction pads with which they attached themselves while they sought entry points. They were hiding in crevices, muttering, unnerving people like her, who'd gone to the toilet unsuspectingly, only to find strange things lurking.

Could they get in? Breach the silver shell? Surely the pressure would drop? They'd be all right. Their bodies would withstand such physical forces. Maybe they didn't have bodies, were just disembodied intelligences trying to communicate. She knew they wanted to talk to her because she'd heard her name, 'Flora', enunciated through crackling static. Spoken, but not the way humans speak. Projected, but not from lungs, more like through pipes or soundboards.

She was aware how long she'd been in the toilet. There'd be people outside, bending their knees to ward off DVT, queuing round into the galley where the cabin crew were organising the next round of snacks and drinks. But she didn't want to go out, to leave the whispering and rustling. They were just starting to get through. 'Flora,' they said again. 'Flora.'

Someone banged on the door and asked, 'You OK in there, ma'am?' She thought it was the blonde one. The mature one with still-shapely legs in laddered tights.

'Yes,' she called. 'Be out soon.'

She bent close to the slot and whispered, 'Don't go away. Flora will be back,' then slid the door open, lowering her head to avoid the accusing stares. Back in her seat, she wrapped herself in the maroon blanket. She'd wait. They'd contact her again.

A Fitting End—Helen Beckett

Sally picked up the lid of the urn and stared at the powdery, grey ash inside. Incredible to think that a person could be reduced to so little. They'd been married for nearly eighteen years, although she'd not seen him for the last twelve. She'd never been to visit.

Remembering what someone had once said about everything having a price, she'd put the urn and its dubious contents for sale on an online auction site, thinking that maybe a theatre or film company might want it as a prop. She hadn't set a reserve but still the bloody thing hadn't sold. She shook her head. 'Wha' the 'eck am I supposed tuh do with the ol' devil now?'

A neighbour had suggested burying the urn at the back of the garden but there was no way he was going anywhere near the kids. She gagged at the very thought. She'd gone through the house like a dose of salts afterwards, removing every trace of him. She'd started with his 'study'; thankfully his laptop and phone had already been taken away.

Something her dad had said when she'd told him suddenly came to mind. She grabbed the urn and pounded up the stairs. She held the urn above the toilet and watched with a delicious sense of closure as a stream of incinerated evil trickled down, spreading its pollution on the porcelain and water below, like an oil slick over the sea. Thumping the bottom of the urn to make sure that there wasn't a single speck of him left, she pushed the handle.

A smile played around her lips as the cascade of water flushed all evidence of his miserable existence into the sewer below. Dad had been right—'I allus said he was a reight piece of shit.'

A Good Old Rodeo Never Hurt Anyone—
Anne Howkins

Driving for an hour along linear blacktop echoed in dark storm clouds. Gunning the pickup, Wendy says we won't get wet. Dale sits in the passenger seat the same way he lounges in his veranda rocker, while Wendy shoes horses, feeds the bull, milks the cow, churns yellow butter so rich it makes me gag. Paul talks, spinning his tales of derring-do the same way he does in the pub.

Rangy tanned cowboys leaning against the arena fence, displaying themselves in working blue denim, tightened at the crotch by fringed chaps, signposted with huge silver buckles. Paul watches blonde teenagers gallop golden horses around the arena, their hair and the paraded stars and stripes flying behind them. I hand him a beer. He says *God you're gorgeous* without turning his head.

White-faced calf bolting, jolted skywards as the lasso tightens around its neck. Cowboy out of the saddle running through the dust before the calf hits the deck. The roan mare knows her job, backs away, keeps the line tight as the calf is trussed and the cowboy punches the air. We watch more calves fail to evade the flying rope. Each time Paul is amazed the whole thing takes less than ten seconds. For months he will relate this fact to anyone listening.

Paul refusing to join the line dancing, standing at the bar downing bourbon the way John Wayne did, letting it set his veins ablaze. Courteous grinning ranch-hands encouraging my wrong-footed grapevines, heel digs and pivots with amiable shared laughter. Dale says I ride horses better than I dance.

Driving back to the ranch, Dale asks if I want to do a bit of cattle work with the sorrel horse, help him bring the heifers in.

I feel the lasso tightening round my neck, wait for the jolt.

Always the Princess Aurora—Safia Sawal

Coming round from that crashed out type of sleep, half dressed, eyelids glued together, mascara smears on her face, her fur-coated tongue cries out for water. She vaguely remembers getting home and what's his name? A decent rower, some uncomfortable fumbling, room spinning as she was pushed back heavily onto the bed, his weight on her, claustrophobic, she was sick. Slam, he was gone.

Showered, percolator bubbling, alone and lonely, Hilary reaches for her phone to humiliate him first. She pauses and smiles at a small metal frame inlaid with coloured glass butterflies, her beautiful mum, a young woman then, laughing at her animated toddler, who appears to be giving a very detailed and serious lecture. Their eyes locked in that moment. Touching her mum's face, she wonders, what story was she telling that could make someone look at her with so much love?

She remembers their early mornings; are all toddlers up so early? They would sneak downstairs 'shush, don't wake daddy'. Her mum, mug of tea and wrapped in a blanket would watch as her wide-awake Hilary, in her tiny pink tutu and silky ballet shoes, would float about the room in a game of make believe, uninterested in the disciplined pointing of toes or positioning of arms. Quietly their favourite ballet music would play and when Hilary tired and thirsty clambered under the blanket for her drink, her mum would tell her all about the beautiful princess Aurora.

They went to see it once; her little legs hung over the end of the big chair, she had clutched the programme so tightly, so happy and excited. She closes her eyes now and her mum squeezes her hand.

Hilary picks up the phone. 'Hi, Mum, what's for dinner?'

A Mind at Peace—Claudia Saalmueller

I sit down on a cushion, cross-legged, placing the palms of my hands on my thighs, closing my eyes. I take a couple of deep breaths, trying to let go of any tension in my body. For a second I have the feeling that I can be totally in the moment, fully aware of my body, my mind and my thoughts. And in that very moment everything around and within me is silent. But then...

Oh, coffee would be nice! Why is there no coffee? It's 5 a.m. Who gets up at 4:30 during their holidays? I must be crazy—am I crazy? My leg hurts already. How long have I been sitting here? No, it's just an itch—am I allowed to scratch my leg? Am I allowed to change my position? COFFEE! Wait! I heard something—a fly? Or was that my stomach? Why is it making that sound? I'm hungry!

I open my left eye slightly, just to see what the others are doing. We are a circle, with everybody concentrating, all eyes shut. Am I the only one suffering? I close my eye again.

Why are the others not moving? Are they better than me? They are better than me. MOTHER! Why am I thinking about my mother? Coffee! Somebody, please have mercy and give me some caffeine!

I hear the sound of a singing bowl. *Thank God it's over.* The woman who is sitting across from me gets up, and we meet at the entrance door.

'Is it your first day here?' she asks. I nod.

'Will I see you around?'

'Oh yes', I answer. 'I'll definitely do that again tomorrow morning'.

Birds of Poland—Jenny Woodhouse

It's only the birds that keep me here. Otherwise I'd be back home in Bavaria. Of course it's good to have a wage, but the job's not up to much. I patrol the perimeter fence on my own for twelve hours every night. I like doing nights. It's colder then, but quiet. A blanket of darkness muffles the rumble and thrum of the works. You could almost imagine there was nothing, nobody inside the fence.

I knock off around dawn. You might think I'd want to get straight to my bed, but you'd be wrong. The sun is showing patchily through the mist, rose shading to gold. I wander towards the Vistula, meandering through the landscape. I sit down, my back against a birch tree. I open my little package of black bread and sausage, and eat my breakfast. The sky brightens and the air warms. The birds are singing already, first the robin, then the blackbirds and the thrushes.

I have my binoculars ready. A woodpecker passes close by, rising and dipping like a Messerschmitt in a dogfight. A snipe feeding in the mud pauses for a moment and utters its clattering call. An eagle soars high overhead.

The air is sweet here, away from the works. On patrol, I can smell the fumes of the processes. Other smells, too, worse. I try not to notice them.

As the day ends the light fades, and I return to my post. The sky fills with a swirling cloud, a murmuration of starlings. They form patterns, disperse, reshape. Finally they roost, a community at peace with itself.

It's the birds that keep me here.

Chewed-up Nails and Dandelion Clouds—
Jamie D. Stacey

They're small and jagged, these nails. Chewed up, like they'll soon cease to exist. From a squirrel, a rare red, that's what I tell myself. After my walk I place them in a jar, preserving them on the bedside table next to your side of the bed.

They're waving with dozens of golden fingers, these dandelions. Soaring, I see their seeds everywhere. Alongside the river I find them huddled together under the sun, these dandelion clouds all wispy and white. I feel their lightness on my skin, shy like a first kiss. After my walk I place them in another jar, these curls and folds that resemble your hair.

They're tough, these pieces of bark, this skin; the white willow droops and sags with age, its branches unfurling over the river like some great yawn before a deep sleep. I wonder at the hours I have sat here now, picking at its bark, leaning in to listen as the wind gives it a voice. I pick away, collecting, until the bark softens and reveals a wrinkled smile. That's what I tell myself. I store it away, this lasting expression, in another jar.

They're fading, these footprints. I plant my feet in the ground beside them, try to walk alongside them once more before fallen leaves hide them and other life grows and replaces them all. I snap photos of them, try to capture these memories before they're forgotten.

They're empty now, these jars; the chewed-up nails and dandelion clouds and tough bark, as well as the blue iris eyes, the voice recording of robins singing at dawn, some freshwater from the river that you used to wet your lips. I lie on the bed and turn to your side, piecing you back together one last time before finally falling asleep.

China White—Fritz Cavelle

There is a line where the Xialao Brook meets the Yangtze River that is as sharp as a butcher's cut. The brook is turmeric yellow, the river industrial grey, the line a churning border between the wild and the tamed.

The Yangtze's banks swarmed black with men made ants, shouldering huge panniers of coal. The skyline bled with smokestack smut above the septic throb of Hades' furnaces. My fortune was here: to teach the Western ways to riches. I am good at this. I'd made my name, my masters in the city trusted me. And they were my future.

Their factories ran for miles, sucking raw materials in and spewing shiny disposables out. In a week I'd made my mark, then...

'I am Ting,' she said. 'Like the bell.' She was a guide, with perfect PLA English. 'I show you.'

We drove in a sheet-metal jeep through a forest of tall, bamboo scaffolding that mapped the emerging city, then out through an ochre moonscape and into leggy, lush woodlands.

'Now we eat? My home. Yes?'

We stopped on a promontory above the Xialao. Her grey-stone village ran in steep steps down to its banks. Around it paddy fields opened like lily pads.

Far to my left a charcoal mushroom billowed above my new industrial home. To my right, a dove-grey smudge hung on the horizon from the city's corporate heat. And before me: a wide twist of golden water, paprika red earth, emerald green jungle and a wide, luminous, colourless sky.

I couldn't step forward. I couldn't step back.

I accept your judgement. I am no longer capable. I cannot fit the mould. Take what you want, say what you wish, but leave me here; here beneath the awning of China white.

Cold Fish—Anne Cuthbert

Everywhere I look, there are fish. In the plaster decoration of the columns, woven silkily into tapestries on the walls, cunningly carved into the oaken backs of chairs, painted boldly onto earthenware jugs of ale. Fish, too, on the trestle tables. Trout and tench lie on platters, salmon in kettles, perch and carp on pewter plates. Sprinkled with samphire, salt cod and mackerel swim in green sauce. In the centre, a giant dish of lampreys.

At the head of the table, presiding over everything, the Prime Warden of the Worshipful Company of Fishmongers sits, looking for all the world like a lamprey himself. Those flat eyes, the grey chinless face, that gaping mouth with yellow snaggle teeth. He looks across with what he thinks is a smile. I see it for what it really is. He wishes to clamp that funnel mouth on me, rub his clammy body against mine. I have been instructed to be polite so I suppress a shudder, nod then look away.

I fix my eyes on a great tapestry which shows the coat of arms of this respected guild. In the centre, there's a crown with leaping dolphins. To the left, an armoured merman bears a falchion, to the right, a mermaid holds a mirror. This is how he would have me, I think—a mermaid upon land, unable to run. Her hair is unloosed in a coppery curtain, swept back from naked breasts between which rests a heavy jewel on a golden chain. I touch the smooth ruby at my neck, a gift bought with salty coins and given to my father as bait. I am in the wicker trap already, waiting for the hand to reach in and grasp me round the gills.

Fox—Sheila Blackburn

Cold, quiet night.

Curtains closed against a pale moon, blue-flickering TV screens, duvet-hills pulled over restless sleepers. Empty, moonlit roads like rivers, where litter-rags flap on hedge and wire. Night workers plough the dull hours before morning—and the red fox prowls.

From the looming, black woods, he moves on silent paws, ears pointed, listening to the night-voices. Across the harvest-rutted fields, wet nose working the aching cold, below steel-sharp stars.

Sleek-sly hunter of the moon-time, he brushes the wayside grasses, his breath a mist of silver. Against shuttered chicken coops he passes, slinking among the shadows, skirting the safety light-pool, smiling at his own resolve. Moves on.

Beyond the shippen, water seeps, unchecked—here the fox pauses, drinks deeply, knows the warm-breathing cows, sweet scent of silage. Sweat of man. Hears the hard metal gun-click of his nightmares—and is gone.

Now, he makes the roadside verge his own, laughs wickedly at the yellow moon. At the stone bridge he pauses, stares down the fire-eyed farm cat. Something moves in the ditch-dampness; something harsh in his night.

Little red fox takes the village road, thinks of food; not prices to be paid, nor prejudice. Feels only grumbling hunger, driving him on. Little red fox on the road: knows death in snares or at the end of a gun barrel…death well-timed but never timely. Knows nothing of things accidental. The flip of a coin, the split second of chance.

Little red fox on the road. Nose quivers. One paw twitches. Engine roar, petrol in the air. Flesh against metal. Animal fear squealing at the darkness—why *here,* tonight..?

Little red fox on the road—returning to earth and his own darkness…

Little red fox on the road—alone and perfect and quite dead.

Freudian Slip—Helen Beckett

Bloody office parties, Becky thought, as she vomited into the toilet. The cold water splashed over her face only helped temporarily. She stumbled towards the bedroom but the thought of Harry drove her to the kitchen instead.

Nursing a mug of coffee, she settled on the sofa and pulled the throw tightly around her. Unwanted images of the night before replayed in her head. They'd already been round a few times—If you had to sleep with someone in the office, who would it be? Who's your girl crush?—when First Loves was suggested as the next topic.

Becky was surprised at how easily the memories had come back to her: walks on the beach; spectacular sunsets; sitting on the handlebars of his bike; laughter. The rest of them were as in love with him as she'd been by the time she'd finished.

'What happened to Adam then, Becs?'

Going to different universities. Working in different cities. Life generally, she supposed or maybe it had always been too perfect to last? She pulled down the neck of her pyjama top and stared at the tattooed name, Adam, that had, since the early hours of this morning, adorned the top of her shoulder.

She woke to the sound of Harry drumming his fingers on the table.

'God, you look a state.' His voice was low and slow. 'Come back to bed but tidy yourself up first.'

Becky locked herself in the bathroom and stared into the mirror. He was right. She did look a sight; her skin was grey, her eyes red. She looked like how she felt. Her gaze slid down to her shoulder. The realisation hit her like yet another slap in the face that it wasn't the tattoo she needed to get rid of.

Good for What Ails You—Lynn Ramsson

1.

What's this mark on your chin? Rowan asked, tracing the wound on her neck with his fingertips.

That's where they tacked my skin open to get the bad out.

Does it hurt?

Not anymore.

It looks painful.

Yes.

Come to Andros when you're better. We'll go fishing.

2.

The skies were cloudless, but the 9-seater from Nassau to Congo Town shuddered and dipped throughout the fifteen-minute flight.

Rowan had sent a man named Theophilus to meet her. Theophilus knew about plants, so he brought a flask of mint tea dosed with allspice leaves to settle her stomach, just in case.

As they rattled past the spindly pines that lined the dirt road to Rowan's lodge, Theophilus talked about the medical properties of the local flora. He gestured to the undergrowth on the side of the road, so she asked him if he knew about other kinds of growths, like the kind that can take over a body.

Theophilus gave her advice, recipes, a warning.

Be careful you respect the chickacharnee.

He slowed down, pointed to the tops of two pine trees, joined in a birds' nest.

Our local imp. He doesn't like outsiders. He looks like an owl, but with long legs. And he lives wherever treetops touch.

3.

The day she noticed another lump, Rowan took her fishing. Then she went for a walk in the forest in search of cascarilla.

Down at the beach, she checked the recipe. After soaking the stems in seawater, she plied the bark away from the slender trunks. She dropped a teaspoon of wood shavings into a mug and buried the rest in the sand as an offering to the chickacharnee.

The bits of wood piled next to her, useless, as her tonic cooled in the hot midday sun.

Hey, Lady!—Anne Cuthbert

We've forgotten the flask, so I'm heading back to the car to collect it. Striding out along the Foreland at Ballantrae, I hear a call.

'Hey, Lady!'

I look across to where the voice is coming from. Standing at the edge of the pebbled beach, Ailsa Craig looming mistily behind him, is a tall figure, grey ponytail, black vest, dark jeans, tattoos twining up arms that are still muscular.

'Hey, Lady!' he repeats, looking directly at me.

My stride falters. I find myself responding to his call. We will ride away together, into the west, my arms clasping his not-quite-run-to-fat waist, my head leaning against his strong back, smelling the sweat and leather, thighs gripping his powerful Kawasaki.

'Hey, Lady!' he calls a third time. I am close to him now. We will ride…

But his gaze is not on me. He is looking down at the grass of the beachside putting green. I look down too, just in time to stop myself from tripping over the small white body running round my legs.

He clips a lead to the poodle's collar and they walk away.

Hitching Down the M5—Bronwen Griffiths

Wind whips down the slip road that leads from the Lydiate Ash roundabout onto the M5. Her mouth is dry, though she has just sipped from a water bottle. She huddles inside the raincoat, shuffles her boots on the gravel, re-arranges her face into a half-smile half-scowl that she hopes will give her the impression of being friendly and tough. She does not feel tough. Only her boots are tough, with their thick soles, the black leather cracked like dried mud.

She sticks out her right arm, her thumb.

A banana lorry pulls up almost immediately. It's a long step up into the cab—her first time inside a truck.

'Where are you going?' The driver seems trustworthy but like her face both may be a lie.

'Bristol.' She's hitched before but never alone. Once, with a friend, a man said if he could kiss one of them, he'd take them further. She said no, yet the friend seemed to think she'd acquiesced. She hadn't. An argument followed. They got out of the car.

The driver offers her a banana. She expects a crude joke. None arrives.

She doesn't need to hitch—her mother gave her the money for the coach fare—so why is she doing this? All she knows is that she loves being out here on the road, the recklessness of it. The fact that there's a boyfriend at the end of the motorway is, for now, of little importance. What she wants is to be up here in the cab, watching the white lines disappearing into the distance; the autumn leaves a blur of rusts, ochres and greens. She wants to be in this cab forever, as the tyres rumble down the asphalt and the diesel fumes belch out into the crystalline air.

Lilith and the Half-Cut Magician—
Mark Kilburn

'Settle, children!' shouted the usher. The lights began to dim.

The seafront theatre was old and spooky. Someone (a ghost, perhaps) pumped the wheezy organ, conjuring an overture for the show to start.

Lilith, the magician's assistant, entered to applause. She was young and wore a basque, fishnets, dainty heels and all the trimmings. She stood alone on stage for a long time, looking like a pornographic photo from the Victorian era. Harry Bingo, the magician, was nowhere to be seen.

At last he stumbled onto the stage, an old bloke in a frayed suit and a kiddies' cowboy hat. Lilith hissed at him from behind her false, ruby red smile.

'Allo boys and girls,' slurred Harry. 'I've 'ad a tipple or two. Can yer tell ?'

He giggled and checked his pockets. 'Gordon Bennett…,' he said, 'I can't find me magic candy.'

He performed a couple of tricks—both fell flat. His preparation was slow; his sleight-of-hand laboured. Somebody booed. Bingo got tetchy.

He regained his composure and announced it was time to saw the beautiful lady in half. Lilith shook her head. 'Not on my nellie!' she said in a strong East European accent.

They had an argument then, right there on stage. 'Come on, Katerina love…' said Harry. 'I've sobered up now, honest.' But it was too late. Lilith walked off. The boys in the audience groaned.

Harry tried again but had an attack of hiccups. His magician's patter creaked like a scuttled schooner. But at least he got some laughs.

When it was all over we ambled along the promenade. A girl who looked like Lilith passed by, swearing in a foreign language. I stood with my sixpenny ice cream, listening to the hiss and rush of the evening tide and Harry Bingo's lonesome tears.

Maternal Instinct—Susan Howe

Elaine was, first and foremost, a mother. Even though her son was thirty years old with the physique of a rugby player, she encouraged him to stay at home until he found the right girl.

Her friends weren't sure she was doing the right thing and enjoyed many discussions about it when Elaine was absent.

'It isn't natural, a man that age living with his mum.'

'But she's done a wonderful job, being both mother *and* father to him.'

'It'll end badly, you'll see. He'll turn out gay—or *worse*!'

Elaine knew, however, that without her watchful eye, he was apt to slide into some odd behaviour. There'd been a number of incidents over the years but she was sure they weren't *all* his fault. She told him repeatedly that the biggest guys had to be extra careful.

'If you see a girl out alone, cross to the other side of the road,' she said, yet again.

'I know, Ma. The big guy always gets the blame, blah blah blah.'

He crossed his feet on the coffee table, then pulled out a pack of cigarettes and dropped the wrapper on the floor. Elaine pushed his legs aside and picked it up before handing him a beer.

At least he was in for the night and she'd get some sleep. Recently his secrecy was unnerving her and she sometimes recoiled when she retrieved his clothes to wash. She'd had to throw one shirt away, soaking it in Bio-Clean first.

She told herself it was a phase. He'd grow out of it. The bloodied earring caught in his sweater *was* an added concern but it had gone now, down a manhole and into the sewers. She would protect her son, whatever the cost.

Well, she reasoned, what decent mother wouldn't?

Moon Mamas of the Silk River Nostoi—Mark Kilburn

Reverend Crisp, magnifying glass in hand, stands on Diglis Bridge.

A veteran of the Lost Order of our Fathers he bows, signals, blesses the evening walkers—members of his imaginary flock.

'Seek and I will bury you; Love and I will couple your hearts; Create and I will minister to your day's end.'

He swivels in favour of the small eyes of silk spun onto the bridge's wrought iron girders, manufactured like prayer wheels above the fragrant river's dream.

His good eye swells in the glass. He asks: are all of His creatures fashioned in His image?

A web intricate as scripture summons him—deadly too (like scripture) for juicy aphids ensnared in these silvery chateaus. Like tiny blowfish their mouths send sticky signals to Moon Mama's secret bedchamber, hidden between the bridge's cross-rail and girth.

The aphids bounce and wriggle (unlike Crisp's Sunday celebrants) rapturous, perhaps, for their invisible maker or else simply eager for their hickory bones to be crushed in a late summer show of repentance.

Crisp kneels, whispers to the spider-goddess. 'Reveal yourself,' he says, and the silk rustles quicker than his good eye can see.

A Moon Mama darts, spins her catch into a ball. Sleek, well proportioned, her rump secretes its wisdom from the median spinner. Her beauty is a joy to behold: her elegance, the deep black of her abdomen, her back patterned with a hoplite shield, her silk stronger than any human twine, binding like communion, the small slits of tarsi attuned to the water's pheromones—a balmy summer's Greek-river banquet.

Crisp sighs in wonder. A blink, a breath—she is gone, the

aphid barrel left hanging like a green coronet set on a pagan throne.

He whispers a prayer of forgiveness, signs a holy cross, walks on…

More Than the Words You Left Me—
Jamie D. Stacey

Man (noun): not a woman, not a boy. Not the tears and buckled knees in the shower. So we're doing this now? Other related terms: 'man up', 'men don't cry', 'be a man'.

A real man takes charge. He's authoritative. He takes risks. Was I a risk, was there no return on your investment? Am I collateral damage? Shows no weakness. Shows no tears. Walks in strides. Holds himself upright. Men are fighters. Men are warriors. They serve, protect; fulfil their duty. Was that you, off to fight in some distant land without us?

Men are castles. Impenetrable, sturdy, grey. Full of dungeons. Full of darkness. Walls, towers, turrets. Distant, isolated, hidden. Men are loners. Is that why you left, was that your excuse, it's her job not yours?

Men work hard. Breadwinners, hard earners. Were you building your business? Your reputation, good station? Were you out making money by the million, did you give us more than what the government and law forced you to?

Reliable, resilient, ready. You weren't ready; was she ready? You had issues you needed to deal with; didn't she? Truthful, kind, loving. You didn't love her; did she love you? And what about me; my mind, my matter, and the small matter of our shared DNA?

Man (noun). How about this? Man: what he wants to be, who he wants to be, despite definitions and DNA. What makes a good man? I'm here aren't I, in this room, at this time of night, holding onto my responsibility as he wets his small tears in my squeezed arms knowing that he's not alone.

Octopi—Catherine Cruse

When I wake up, you are already dead.

I can see you every four seconds in the tiny pinpoint flicker of your laptop light. I loved you so very much.

I think of the bottom of the ocean, all the things you thought I did not know. I think about octopuses—octopi?—eight limbs wrapped around your throat. Breathing tiny bubbles of air like silent screams. I think *octopi* might be right but it doesn't sound right, which is what matters, after all.

The night you told me about her we were in an underground Mexican restaurant, served watery margaritas by an Indian waiter in a sombrero. I wore a pink cardigan and kept tugging the sleeves down over my fingers until it was stained paprika orange. I ordered tacos and taquitos and when they arrived I couldn't tell one from the other.

'I'm really sorry,' you said. When we got married and I pictured the end I thought about soft mattresses and lined faces in dimly lit rooms smelling of boiled vegetables and gravy. We said until death do us part, after all.

Do octopuses mate for life?

I took a photograph of my tacos or maybe my taquitos. It got forty-two likes. My next photograph, I think, will get more.

Afterwards I worried she might show up at the funeral but she had the sense to stay away. Perhaps she thinks you killed yourself. Perhaps, in a way, you did.

I loved you so very much.

Is it octopuses or octopi?

You do understand, don't you? I just really couldn't bear it. I couldn't be divorced. It didn't sound right.

Octopuses sounds right.

That's what matters, after all.

Remember the Murdered Man—
Safia Sawal

It wasn't actually a river, more of a channel coming from the Kennet. It was definitely a corpse though. She'd known about the murder, but when they bought the house it hadn't really registered, not with her and not with John.

For them the brook had been a real selling point, the previous owners were leaving the rowing boat. It was perfect, idyllic and either side of their little stretch two bowing willows whose branches floated on the surface of the water, gliding with the current.

At night she would sit out on the bank, drawn to the water, drawn to where a branch of the willow was stuck, creating a ripple on the surface.

Friends of John's came for a drink. They'd all worked in housing together. 'John this is the brook, the one where your tenant dumped that body.'

She remembered then the terrible senseless murder. The focus had been on the murderer. Even now she could remember everything about him and nothing about the murdered man.

At night she was drawn to the brook, it gurgled where the branch was stuck.

She went to the library and looked at the newspapers from the time, a lot of information on the murderer, not much on the murdered man, but enough she hoped.

At night she was drawn to the brook; the water rippled and gurgled; she looked up at the stars. 'Your name is Imran, you were a taxi driver and you were still young, you had three children: Rohaan, Durnaz and Mizhir; you had a wife, Shehrnaz; your mother and father lived with you. Your family and friends had only good things to say about you. You were a good Muslim. You were murdered for no reason.'

The ripple stopped, the branch sprung free.

Repeat Patterns—Susan Howe

She knits as though she doesn't know what else to do. Knit one, purl one; some things are never forgotten. For you, she mastered every pattern, knitting in enough love for two, to compensate for your father's absence.

She said you were all she had and trapped you within her words.

Then your father's letter arrived from Australia, offering you more than clothes. Sunshine and opportunities.

When you emigrated, you gave your collection of knitwear to Oxfam. Afterwards, she spent her days knitting simple squares for Care Home blankets. Very like the one she's wrapped in now.

Singapore Green—Fritz Cavelle

Serangoon Road at two a.m. is not a place to be if you didn't have some form of Mandarin; I had little. Within the sight of the Sri Veran temple ran an alleyway: a strip of stamped earth with beer-shacks built from stacked crates on one side and a slatted concrete fence faced with shrubbery on the other. Between them stood a line of white plastic tables and stacking chairs. I sat at the same place sucking at a Tiger beer so often that the barkeep would smile, nod and uncap a bottle before I'd settled into my spot.

The ladyboys swaggered past, gorgeous in their black, micro-skirted, business suits. The coffin-sized rooms of the Desker Road brothels lay just a street away but I was here for other things.

I sat there for twenty nights before I saw the business.

A group of regulars, Malays I think, were sitting just two tables away, smoking ferociously, slapping backs and cackling like toucans when they were joined by someone I'd not seen before.

He was short, squat, missing a finger from his left hand and wearing a battered brown leather jacket, even on this sauna of an evening. As he approached from the junction, he crouched beside a cherry laurel as if to tie his shoe and quickly riffled through its leaves, before being embraced by his friends.

Fifteen minutes later, the heady tang of bougainvillea had been clouded by the cat-piss scent of marijuana.

On the twenty-first night the bush had been uprooted and I drank for free.

Months later I found an edition of the New Straits Times wedged into my letterbox. Deep within its folds the 'Court & Crimes' section reported that 'Stubby' Tsang had been hanged.

Next job: Huddersfield.

...So,—Mark Rogers

...So, the Boy, often sat at his GranPop's feet, as the old man busied himself with pencil and paper.

They sit now, beneath the only apple tree in the old man's garden. It, protecting them from the worst effects of a harsh midday sun.

'I first discovered I could draw a perfect circle when I was a little older than you,' he says to the Boy, scrunched at the foot of his chair.

And with elderly hand, he passes a newly drawn circle to his grandson, who dutifully, places that with the others.

The Boy considers his grandfather's tone a little harsh, but has learnt to ride with the old man's temper and maintain a cheery aspect rather than sulk. 'That's twelve this morning, GranPops,' confirms the little fella. 'Market day I'll sell them at the roadside, we can eat well that day, GranPops. Figs, I'll buy figs,' and the old man nods, once, twice, three times as he considers one more drawing, pre-lunch.

Deep in thought he tap tap taps his pencil, a 4B graphite, Palomino Blackwing 602, one of a box set, provided as a gift, by his friend Carol last spring.

'For your birthday,' she said, kissing his head. He's heard she didn't make it through the bitter winter, and now misses her company, her shy caress.

He pushes out a sheet of blinding white Strathmore, stretches it out across his drawing table, relishes the smoothness. Places a palm down against the cool crisp white, and stares up at the ceaseless sun, it, penetrating the apple-heavy canopy.

'We could have fish today, GranPops,' says the Boy. 'I brought sardines with me, fresh from the harbour. Straight from the nets, like you told me.'

And the old man, unflinching, casts his pencil, forming a perfect circle…

So Long Solar—Simon Linter

A man found a mirror in the desert that reflected the sky. A tumbleweed drifted past backwards, in reverse, dropping seeds as it tumbled. A backdrop of mountains on the horizon gave the man some hope as he brushed away the dusty sand, gazed into the mirror, shaggy beard, unruly eyebrows, sweat, the worry, stress lines on the forehead, where had he put his water? No time to be vain, the picture behind him said something else. A tree that looked like a flag; a black flag made up of smoke, dust, fumes, carbon, it blew in the wind as the tumbleweed had, dropping its pollution into the off-blue sky, towards the backdrop of mountains, but were they mountains? The bumps on the horizon. They were getting larger, moving towards him, towards the black flag in the mirror, flashing blue lights and animals on leads, breath on the mirror; he was still alive, thank goodness. The black flag kept flapping until its smoke had all but gone with just the flagpole remaining. He licked his lips, grit in the mouth, where had he put his water? He collapsed, the mirror picking up the bald spot on his head that he was unaware of, and watched the lumps, the people, the scientists, the police, get closer, closer, to his answer, in the desert, where the sun beat down on those tumbleweeds, on the man, now slumped, smiling, muttering to himself that this is the where the answer is, in the mirror, if they would only look.

The Heatwave of 1957—Safia Sawal

The heat has been intense, the days long. Pauline's days stretch in front of her, she watches the seconds, minutes, hours, waiting for the clock to tick forward. There's no breeze, the air is suffocating.

Pauline stares at William's newspaper; he works the day shift, making French cars. She sits opposite his empty plate pouring a lukewarm tea, she flicks through his newspaper: a housewife in her frilly white pinny dances with her vacuum cleaner, while another beams enthusiastically at the brightness of OMO as she stands proudly by her twin tub with mangle.

Pauline doesn't have these things and William doesn't have a French car. He is a quiet man, polite, a proper gentleman. He works hard, he's never late and he's never ill. William provides.

It happened so quickly, she didn't have the right feelings; her mother said it would come in time. 'He's a good man.' Pauline hated his body, his clumsy fingers. The good man, the quiet man, knew this; it excited him. Every night he would grab her to him, sometimes she begged, 'Not tonight,' but this excited him more. Pauline learnt to keep quiet.

Every day Pauline walks for miles; not today, the air is stifling. A storm is coming.

It has been forty years since that particular storm and today is Pauline's last day at work, she's had some beautiful gifts and flowers.

'I started here that year when we had the heatwave, you won't remember—I doubt most of you were born—well there were some terrible storms and I lost my Bill. He was such a good man, a quiet man, struck by lightning on his way home from the factory. I thank God he didn't suffer.'

The Man I Love—John Holland

The man I love lies in his bed in the lounge. He wears pyjamas and disposable pants.

I cannot stay with him all the time.

When I return to the room, the man I love points at the pants on the floor. I wash him down—including his hair and the excrement from beneath his finger nails—strip the bed and re-make it before dressing him in clean pyjamas and new disposable pants.

This happens most days. The man I love can no longer say thank you.

But I do not need him to.

The Monument—Charlotte Pinkney

The monument stood on the horizon. No one remembered it appearing; equally, no one agreed that it had been there all along. Nonetheless, the town accepted it as one of their own. The monument had a curious feature. No matter how close you got to it, it seemed the same distance away, and so the casual visitor was discouraged and for much of the year it stood alone. On Midsummer's Eve, however, it pulled like a tongue to a missing tooth: probing, impossible to resist. Above all, unconscious. Each year, it rose as a task for each person in the town. As the sun began to set, everyone would set down what they were doing, nod to anyone about, and turn their attention to the monument. In the setting sun, the monument cast a long shadow over the town, creating a road along which the people walked. Although there was no distinct order when the walk began, by the time they reached the monument, two lines formed as each person paired off. Twenty-seven pairs took their place and waited. Any person asked would have been unable to answer why they waited, except that they must; yet each person would be greatly relieved to have waited for nothing. A shiver passed through the crowd and one pair stepped forward. Facing the monument, the town to their backs, they listened.

You accepted me among you long ago. I thank you. Now it is time for you to thank me.

And the pair fell to the floor in a frenzied attack. Each impassive face watched as the pair wrestled, strangled, scratched, until one stood victorious. Blood seeped towards the monument and, as it shuddered, the crowd returned to the town, unconcerned and unknowing.

The Tale of Hickory Dickory—Polly Caley

In an instant he was on me, pinning me to the floor. I couldn't breathe. Grinning, he released me, only to take a swipe at me. My thumping heart felt ready to leap free from my chest.

A girl came and saw. She started shrieking and yelling. I seized my chance and somehow managed to run.

I hid behind the refrigerator, sticky with blood. When I stopped trembling, I noticed an abundance of crumbs. I ate hungrily to regain strength.

The girl, my angel, bent down crossly, scooped up the cat and cast him out. He screeched furiously.

As I stuffed my cheeks, the old hickory clock struck one. We were meant to meet under it. The chime signalled I was already very late. He'd promised nirvana—there wasn't a moment to lose. I worried he'd change his mind about sharing the haul.

I fled across the kitchen and into the hallway. But then I made the awful discovery. More bloodshed.

Behind the large clock lay Dickory, unmoving, his neck snapped. I quivered to the tips of my whiskers. His glassy eyes stared back. I slumped against him, feeling hopeless, then gradually took in the surrounding scene. He had delivered on his promise.

Dickory had managed to dislodge large lumps of marzipan and fat chunks of cheese from most of the traps, before meeting this tragic last one. Good ole Dickory had not put his neck out in vain! There was enough to satisfy all of our bellies for days on end.

I recalled something my father always used to say and scratched it hurriedly into the hardwood clock, lest we forget the tale of Hickory Dickory:

'The early bird may catch the worm, but it's the late mouse that gets the cheese. Eat and remember him.'

The Voices Inside—Kevin Brooke

Rumpelstiltskin had always envied Pinocchio, the wooden boy who would forever be known as the good guy.

'How do you make people like you?' Rumpelstiltskin asked, as they entered the fairy-tale forest.

'By doing nice things,' Pinocchio answered, 'and listening to the little voices inside.'

Rumpelstiltskin didn't really know what he meant but followed him through the forest until they came to a cottage. Smoke swirled from its chimney and three bears headed towards the front door.

'Trust your conscience,' Pinocchio said, 'and do the right thing.'

Rumpelstiltskin shrugged. 'There's a girl inside your house,' he cried. 'She's robbing your food, breaking your furniture and sleeping in your beds.'

Pleased with himself, Rumpelstiltskin turned to Pinocchio who was shaking his head. 'Try listening to the little voice next time,' he said. 'Not the loud, angry one.'

Increasingly confused, Rumpelstiltskin carried on along the path and soon met a wolf.

'Have you seen a girl in a red cloak?' the wolf asked.

Rumpelstiltskin was about to tell him about the flash of red he'd seen amongst the trees, when a little voice squeezed its way past the angry one.

'No,' he replied. 'I haven't seen a thing.'

'That's better,' Pinocchio said. 'Let's try one more.'

As they headed along the path, they came to a bridge on which three goats were standing. Rumpelstiltskin was about to summon the troll when a little voice told him to find a safer route and, together with the goats, he waded across the river. By the time he reached the opposite bank, however, his feet were wet and cold, his patience spent.

'Oh, to be warm,' he said, when he found the dying embers of a bonfire underneath a tree. Ignoring the little voice, he grabbed the wooden boy and threw him onto the fire.

Thoughts of a Woman Scorned—
Jan Baynham

I had no option, agápi mou[1]. You wouldn't be happy giving up the life we had together. Our rich friends from Athens, thrilling trips through the psychadelic universe, the buzz of securing a deal, then frittering away the proceeds. I've set you free. *He*'ll pay for this. Nobody will believe that you, the handsome art tutor everyone adores, would kill himself. The 'suicide' note hints of the row between you; everyone saw the mess he made of your face. He'll be prime suspect, I made sure of that. That's why I planted the packet of orange sunshine pills next to you. Re-addressed it to him. Clever, eh? And the knife? That was easily done. I slipped into the woodturner's studio when he was outside talking to that pretty student of yours and took it from his work bench. No, he'll be sorry he ever tried to get you to come clean about 'our little *business*'.

I hated what I had to do to you. Nearly didn't go through with it. But I made sure we had a good time before you slipped into a deep sleep. At our favourite place for making love. Under our special olive tree. One last time, the best ever. You never tasted what was in the raki. You fell asleep so fast. I slit your vein as quickly as I could. That wasn't hard for me, was it, with *my* past history? There was no hiding the scars from you that first time we got together. You were the only person I'd told about the real reason for them. Before I left you, bleeding and your life draining away, I pulled your fingers around the note and scattered the pills.

Good-bye, Stavros. Your brother's going away for a very long time!

---

[1] *agápi mou—my love*

Toast—Rebecca West

'I'd like to report a murder,' said the blood splattered old man, leaning heavily on his walking stick as he lowered himself onto the plastic chair.

'OK, sir, if I could just get some basic details,' said the detective.

'Walter Eastly, age ninety-eight, the deceased is on my kitchen floor. 22 Park Street, no need for an ambulance,' he said glancing at his watch. 'Albert's been dead well over an hour, it's quite a walk from there you know.'

'Right, sir, do you know why anyone would want to harm him?'

'Oh plenty of people would, he could be a bit of a scoundrel really. He was the youngest in our family, utterly spoiled by our mother, stole my pocket money growing up but never admitted it, even stole my girlfriend in 1942 the bastard. Never bought a round at the pub, and certainly didn't do his share when Dad got dementia. Not exactly a good man but you can't choose your family I suppose.'

'Right, sir, if we could get back to what happened today.'

'Well he's been staying with me this past week. Every morning he changed the toaster settings to number four, now I'm sure I don't need to tell you that's essentially charcoaled bread. Unfathomably he never turned the dial back when he'd finished despite my numerous requests. Three times this week I've accidently burnt my toast. So, I'm afraid in a fit of rage I stabbed him.'

'It sounds like you have quite a history with your brother, would you say this incident was the culmination of a long running family tension?'

'Not in the slightest, sir, I've long since accepted Albert's faults, this was purely about the toast.'

Tumbling Sailor—Roz Levens

Everything looks better in candlelight they say. It's not true. The bloated body gleamed dull white in the gloom, flickering shadows from the candles making it shift and move.

The canvas shroud was pulled close by the sailmaker, as he stitched the sailor into his final overcoat, the last stitch, as traditional, going through the boy's nose to check he wasn't faking.

We knew he wasn't, of course. We'd all seen him plummet from the rigging, heard his scream, watched him drop like a stone into the green depths of the dark, unforgiving sea.

From that height, it's said, hitting water is the same as hitting rock. He'd gone in feet first, the impact of the water tearing his boots clean off their soles, forcing the leather up his legs, leaving his feet bare and strangely pale.

'Death is nothing at all,' said the Captain, as the plank was tilted and the boy fell, for a second time, beneath the waves.

'This is merely his deliverance into the Lord's care.'

I thought about the tumbling sailor often as I was sent up to the crow's nest as lookout. War seemed far away, and far less dangerous than the coarse rigging, the tarred surface slick in the rain and spray. Life below decks was hard for a boy.

I was never entirely certain that he didn't jump.

Unravelling You—Georgie Bull

When you love someone, you know everything about them.

I know that you like your bagels toasted. I know that you can't write without coffee, and that you can't clean the house without blasting cheesy 80's pop on full volume.

Over the months, I've observed your funny habits, connected the dots to unhealthy patterns and unravelled your insecurities.

It worries me how much you obsess over your weight. It's needless—from the moment I first saw you, I thought you were perfect.

But you think you're too big. I've watched you stand in front of the mirror, examining your body from all angles, lips twisted with disgust.

We'll have to work on your binge-eating habit. You make salads for work lunches and lovingly craft healthy dinners—but as soon as you're upset, it's straight for the biscuit tin.

I think I can help you beat this. By being the observer, I can see things that aren't so obvious to you, the victim.

It's your sister that's to blame for this hatred of your own body. Don't tell me you haven't noticed how she never fails to mention that a new outfit is a size 0? Remember last Christmas, when she gave you a jumper two sizes too big? Do you really believe that was an accident?

She's toxic and it's drowning you. But don't worry—starting tonight, I'm going to help you gain control back over your life.

You're going to be a bit late. I can tell. You've been standing at the mirror for over half an hour and haven't dried your hair yet. I'll have to get going now to keep our reservation, but when you do finally arrive, flustered and stressed, I'll have your favourite drink ready and waiting.

I can't wait to finally meet you.

Unsleeping the Dead—Bronwen Griffiths

I'm screaming a scream to un-sleep the dead in the graveyard close to the house, to wake my brother yet unborn, my howling enough to scare the owls in the trees, to flatten the ears of the night-cats slinking along the road towards the bridge, to cause the geese next door to hiss, the bats to veer into the steeple. My tiny fists are clenched, my skin is the colour of the apples falling in the orchards of the village, my face as puckered as the old man who cleans the street on Mondays and now my mother is running fearful up the steep and winding stairs—stairs I, dizzy with flu, will one day tumble down, hitting my head on the piano I will so hate playing.

My mother lifts me from the cot. There is a sudden stink, an almost dropping, the softness of my mother's swollen stomach and the rebellion is dissipated, like a crowd slipping away from the steps of the court after the verdict.

For now, I will let it be known when I am not happy. I have not yet learned the art of politeness, the compromises that I will make.

Via Dolorosa—Brian Comber

Cardinal Rossi passes through the college like a knife through smoke, for thirty days he has written Canon law on the limitations of apostates. They can no more cross sanctified soil nor claim rights to property; this will take effect at Michaelmas, it is his will. He hurries from Compline through the cloisters, feeling fear at his back, he knows, plain as a candle, that his adversary the devil walks the earth like a roaring lion. He studies the anatomy prints in the restricted library, reasoning that the ache he feels may rest, not in his eternal soul but in the ventricles of his heart, he looks, with the curiosity of a cartographer seeking the location of immorality in terra incognita. He skips along the passage to his cell where his boy is sleeping. In an era of faith, just men, with the validation of the Creed, may live untroubled, he writes; the boy stirs. He longs to dance like the others; when his glass brims he watches maids with furtive glances and wonders at the nature of joy. Has it physical being, could the physician Dr Tulp point to it? The carnal world is mysterious, he grapples with the rational as he is a fanatically reasonable man, but his soul rots, like carrion. When he is woken by plain chant from the floor below and the bird song swells, he stares at his single chair and bowl, knowing that he is untethered, barely there. He toys with a caged linnet; for days he has denied it food to see how much it will bear...

...and I, four centuries later, researching his life, understand how tradition sustained dogma long after the argument was lost because the Cardinal, in the torments of sin, had felt the devil's breath on his neck.

Virgin Territory—Helen Beckett

Settling further back into the seat, I press my foot down on the accelerator. I never listen to music in the car, preferring instead the varying sounds the tyres make on the different road surfaces or the deep bass growl of the engine that rises to an urgent scream as I red-line it on a particularly inviting stretch of open road. I find I'm holding my breath, anticipating the three-kilometre stretch of dual carriageway being opened today.

There are so few who understand my passion. Take the girl at the party last week. Her eyes had darted around the room, sending out distress signals, as I'd tried to explain the vaguely erotic thrill of it. I'd been wasting my time with her and the lack of attraction had been mutual. But I think the BMW driver understands. I don't normally rate BMW drivers, find them too aggressive, but this one had been surprisingly nice. I check my appearance in the rear-view mirror, run my fingers through short, dark hair.

As a boy, I'd loved reading about explorers who'd sailed into the unknown. Being one of the first to drive onto virgin tarmac, with its pristine markings, does not compare but it still gives me a faint echo of the thrill, if not the terror, that those brave men must have felt.

I drive to where men in suits, totally unsuited to the weather, are congratulating each other. I silently urge them to move over to the ribbon that shows, yet blocks my way. There's a loud beep. In the mirror I watch the big, black BMW pull up close behind me. I raise a hand in acknowledgement, my heart pounding at the smile that inches along the man's lips and up into the welcoming pools of his deep, brown eyes.

What is in Your Fridge?—Steve Clough

She opened the fridge, the light blinding her for just a moment, the cold air chilling her through the thin nightdress—this was a gruesome time to be up, but her appointment was this morning. The head had continued to ooze liquid all over the base, and his expression was becoming more grotesque by the day. She took out some milk and made her breakfast cereal quietly.

As the coffee brewed, she returned to the bedroom to dress. The hand on the floor no longer worried her, but it would take some more time before she was really prepared to throw it out. She might have to get the ring off first. The bin men had taken the rest of the body last week. Unknowingly, of course.

'Kitchen waste' was such an expansive term.

She would need to go shopping at some point, and would need the space in the fridge. But another week—she would be OK. She checked the calendar for the time of her appointment—half past—she still had time to do her makeup.

'Hello, Jessica,' that was Bernice, cheerful as usual. 'How are things?'

'Oh, erm, much the same.'

'I just want to pick up from your last session where you explained that you felt your marriage was probably all but over. I wondered how you felt about that now?'

'He left me last week. I haven't heard a thing from him since. I would say it is all over.'

When Falling Over becomes Having a Fall—Brian Comber

Mrs Eliot had known fear and joy when she'd been part of the protests at Greenham Common air base. She'd worried about being arrested but had felt a headiness of defiance against something she knew was wrong. She'd talked to many women, across campfires, about how the personal became the political. Her career survived but her view of what unchallenged authority can do was utterly changed by her experiences; she'd also learned to sing.

Mrs Eliot remembered locking arms in a human chain with a sobbing woman and being pulled apart by a uniformed man who said, 'You should be at home, love, your old man wants his tea,' and felt her anger rise up.

She maintained her fury in the following years; she felt there was so much injustice. She often confronted people, but felt that generally people argued along reasonable lines and that consensus could often be achieved, more recently however disagreement always seemed to end in abuse. Mrs Eliot realised that she became invisible with age; bullies who'd stared her in the eyes started to see past her, it was what happened.

One afternoon in her garden she tripped on a bucket and found she couldn't get up; she shivered as the sky darkened until eventually her neighbour, returning from work, heard her shouts.

As she was wheeled into Casualty the ambulance man said to a nurse that she'd had a fall and someone said, 'Bless.' Throughout my life, she thought, I've had 'you're not going out in that', 'women can't be engineers', 'be polite' and now this.

Mrs Eliot heard, 'Come on, Alice dear,' and when she was called 'darling' she knew she'd another fight on her hands.

'Is there anyone you'd like us to speak to?' someone

asked.

'Well you could try me,' she replied.

Woman Driving, Man Sleeping—
John Holland

The map rests on her knee as she drives. She twists the radio dial but no sound emerges. He stays locked in his dreams.

She turns to look at him—at the scar, a highway from the corner of his mouth to the tip of his chin. She thinks about how it tastes on her lips, on her tongue. How it makes her feel inside.

'I might kiss you first,' she says over the thrum of the engine. Then takes the knife from the glove compartment and feels its weight in her hand. Presses the blade into her skin to test its sharpness.

Authors' Biographies

Ann Cuthbert enjoys writing and performing with the Tees Women Poets. Her work has appeared widely on-line and in print. Her chapbook, *Watching a Heron with Davey*, is published by Black Light Engine Room Press. She has been highly commended twice in the Crossing the Tees short story competition.

Anne Howkins has been writing flash fiction for a couple of years, and finds the short form somewhat addictive. Her work has been published by *Lunate*, *Reflex*, *Retreat West*, *Flash 500* and has appeared in various anthologies. When not writing, or working, she rides her pony and needle-felts.

Brian Comber lives in Worcestershire and writes poems and short stories, performing occasionally at Worcester spoken word events. Brian has had flash fiction published in Black Pear Press anthologies; he's also had poetry published online with *Picaroon Poetry*, *Prole Poetry*, *The Beach Hut*, *The Gentian* journal, *Re-side* and *Feral Poetry*. He walks in the countryside quite a lot, particularly when he can't think what to write.

Bronwen Griffiths is the author of two published novels, *A Bird in the House* and *Here Casts No Shadow*, and two collections of flash fiction, *Not Here, Not Us – stories of Syria* and *Listen with Mother*. She lives in East Sussex, UK.

Catherine Cruse is a freelance writer and English Literature graduate from Royal Holloway, University of London. She came second in the FlashFiction500 competition 2018 and has had a number of short stories and poems published in anthologies. She is currently working on a novel.

Charlotte (Charli) Pinkney grew up in Malvern and lived there until she moved for university. As such, in a way a lot of her writing reflects the hills and Worcestershire itself. She enjoys writing horror and fantasy, as it allows for a lot of vivid description and exploring the human experience. She hopes to publish a short story collection soon on these themes. She can be contacted at charlipinkney@gmail.com

Claudia Saalmueller is a performing arts teacher and yoga instructor. She attended the Ludwig Maximilians University in Munich, Germany and holds a master degree in theatre sciences. Her work includes several theatre and show productions and regular classes at public schools.

Fritz Cavelle After a short but successful career on the building sites of Birmingham Fritz travelled the world as an IT consultant before settling down in Worcester. He now lives as a semi-recluse in a deconsecrated church, only emerging to shout at those kind enough to listen or Jehovah's Witnesses.

Georgie Bull is a PR executive by day and fiction writer by night. She has a first-class degree in drama and screenwriting, and worked as a freelance copywriter, scriptwriter and performance artist before going into PR. Her short stories and flash fictions have appeared in numerous anthologies and her first independently published short story collection, *Voices*, was released in 2019. As a scriptwriter and performance artist, she took work to some of the most prominent art platforms and venues including Royal Vauxhall Tavern in London and Emergency festival in Manchester. She is now working on her debut novel, a second short story collection and a childrens' book.
https://www.georgiebull.com
Email: georginabull@outlook.com

Helen Beckett Two of Helen's flashes were shortlisted in the 2017 LitFest Flash Fiction competition and three were included in the 2019 anthology. She's hoping that her lucky streak will continue in 2020. Helen is still working on her novel and is hoping that this is the year when it will finally be finished.

Holly Yuille writes fiction and poetry that is sweet, dark and unexpected. Holly has performed at several spoken word events in Worcester. She was the winner of the 2019 Worcestershire LitFest Flash Fiction Slam and was shortlisted for the 2018 John O'Connor Short Story Competition.

Jamie D Stacey is a part-time writer and full-time father. An avid writer of flash fiction and aspiring novelist (working on that debut!), he is drawn to stories that empathise and empower. He's also just joined twitter: @JamieDStacey1.

Jan Baynham, from Cardiff, has recently had two novels published this year. A member of the RNA and the SoA, her first collection of short stories was published in 2019. Follow her on her Jan Baynham Writer Facebook page and on Twitter @JanBaynham where she runs a fortnightly writing blog,
https://janbaynham.blogspot.com/

Jenny Woodhouse began to write seriously after she retired. She studied creative writing with the Open University. Her output has shrunk from novel to short stories and she now writes mainly flash. Addiction to the Ad Hoc Fiction 150-word challenge makes her afraid of shrinking further, like Alice.

John Holland is a multi-prize winning short fiction author from Gloucestershire in the UK. His work is widely published in anthologies and online. John also runs Stroud Short Stories. His website is johnhollandwrites.com He's on Twitter @JohnHol88897218

Kathryn Barton left school as soon as possible, only too happy to hang up her slate and chalk, vowing to eschew any form of further education, but always wanting to write. A decade ago Kathryn made a complete volte face, now possesses a BA (Hons) and an MA (Distinction) in Creative Writing and is a Master of Philosophy. For the MPhil she produced a collection of short stories set in the New Forest, together with an academic thesis. Kathryn prefers to write light humorous pieces: she would rather like to be the next P G Wodehouse.

Kevin Brooke writes mainly for young people and is the Young Writer Ambassador at Worcestershire LitFest. He has two books published by Black Pear Press, namely, *Jimmy Cricket* and *Max and Luchia: The Game Makers* and is currently spending far too much time on a Young Adult novel that focuses on the theme of anti-violence. It will be called *The Objectors*.

Lynn Ramsson, born in Bangkok and raised near Washington, DC, lived in Los Angeles before moving to the UK five years ago. Lynn is a freelance writer and editor, and she lives with her family and two naughty whippets named Bruno and Genevieve in Hove.

Mark Kilburn was born in Birmingham and lived for a number of years in Scandinavia. Between 1996-98 he was writer in residence at the City Open Theatre, Arhus, Denmark and in 2001 he was awarded a Canongate Prize for fiction. In 2012 he won the AbcTales poetry competition and in 2020 was placed first in the Cerasus Poetry Olympics competition. His novel, *Hawk Island*, is available from electronpress.com

Mark Rogers has been writing and attending open mic spoken word events for a couple of years, headlining at three events. He has two published books: ....*So, 50* and ....*So, much better....* both available through lulu.com. He refers to his stuff as his vinaigrettes; sour little tales.

Polly Caley is the schoolchildren's mum who leads an exciting double life. For when Polly picks up a pen, an amazing transformation occurs. Polly is not Bananaman, but is ever alert for the call to fiction!

Rebecca Klassen is a masters student at the University of Gloucestershire, currently studying Creative and Critical Writing. Rebecca has had publications in *Graffiti* magazine and Tintern Abbey's anthology *Ways to Peace*. She was awarded a prize at the Coleford Festival of Words 2018 competition.

Rebecca West grew up in Yorkshire before moving to Perth, Australia in her twenties where she now lives with her husband and two young sons. She has had several short stories published and is currently working on a novella. When not writing she enjoys running by the coast.

Roz Levens lives in Evesham. Her first novel *Pack of Lies* has just been published, and she's chuffed to little mint balls about it. She likes open mic nights, walking the dog and eating cake, not necessarily in that order. She's working on novels number two, three and four and lives in a state of permanent confusion.

Safia Sawal has been attending creative writing courses and workshops for a few years and feels that she has been inspired to find more creativity in her work. Her biggest excuse to herself for not writing is time, fitting in her writing between two jobs, family and hours of peaceful dog walking.

Sheila Blackburn is a retired primary teacher, loves writing and has had magazine stories published, plus children's reading books. Flash fiction is a big challenge for her and she always enjoys the word target. Living in a rural setting, 'Fox' is a locally inspired story.

Simon Linter lives in Stockholm, Sweden, but comes from England. He has an MA in creative writing and has had work published by *Aesthetica*, *Two Thirds North* and *Litro Magazine*. He has written several books and has worked as a journalist.

Steve Clough is fifty-seven, works in software development, and has been writing for seven years. He has self-published one work and is seeking an agent for his most recent one. He is a member of a writing group who loved this piece! stevecloud@gmail.com

Susan Howe's short stories and flash fictions have been published and placed in competitions many times. A proud but displaced Yorkshirewoman, brevity is in her DNA.

Yvonne Clarke lives in Chichester, West Sussex but has family living in Worcester. She worked for a number of publishers as an editor throughout her life before working as an English teacher. She loves writing flash fiction, music, cycling, gardening, and is passionate about the environment and animal welfare.